W9-BAG-248

My
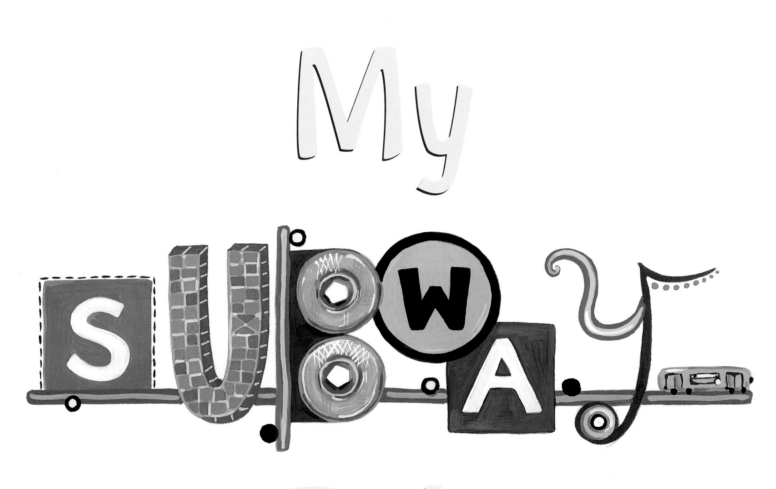
SUBWAY
Ride

FOR NATALIA BELÉN, P. J. AND J. S.
FOR MY MOTHER, S. A.

First Edition
14 13 12 11   11 10 9 8

Text © 2004 Jacobs and Swender, Inc.
Illustrations © 2004 Selina Alko

All rights reserved. No part of this book may be reproduced by any means whatsoever without written permission from the publisher, except brief portions quoted for purpose of review.

Published in conjunction with the New York Transit Museum.

Published by
Gibbs Smith, Publisher
P.O. Box 667
Layton, Utah 84041

Orders: 1.800.748.5439
www.gibbs-smith.com

Designed by Dawn DeVries Sokol
Manufacture in Shenzhen, China, in July 2011 by Toppan Printing

Library of Congress Cataloging-in-Publication Data

Jacobs, Paul DuBois.
My subway ride / Paul DuBois Jacobs and Jennifer Swender ;
illustrations by Selina Alko.—1st ed.
p. cm.
Summary: Relates the sights and sounds of a subway ride through the boroughs of New York City.
ISBN 10: 1-58685-357-0 : ISBN 13: 978-1-58685-357-0
[1. Subways—Fiction. 2. New York (N.Y.)—Fiction.] I. Swender, Jennifer. II. Alko, Selina, ill. III. Title.
PZ7.J15252My 2004
[E]—dc 22
                    2004005052

My Subway Ride

PAUL DUBOIS JACOBS AND JENNIFER SWENDER

Illustrations by Selina Alko

Gibbs Smith, Publisher
Salt Lake City

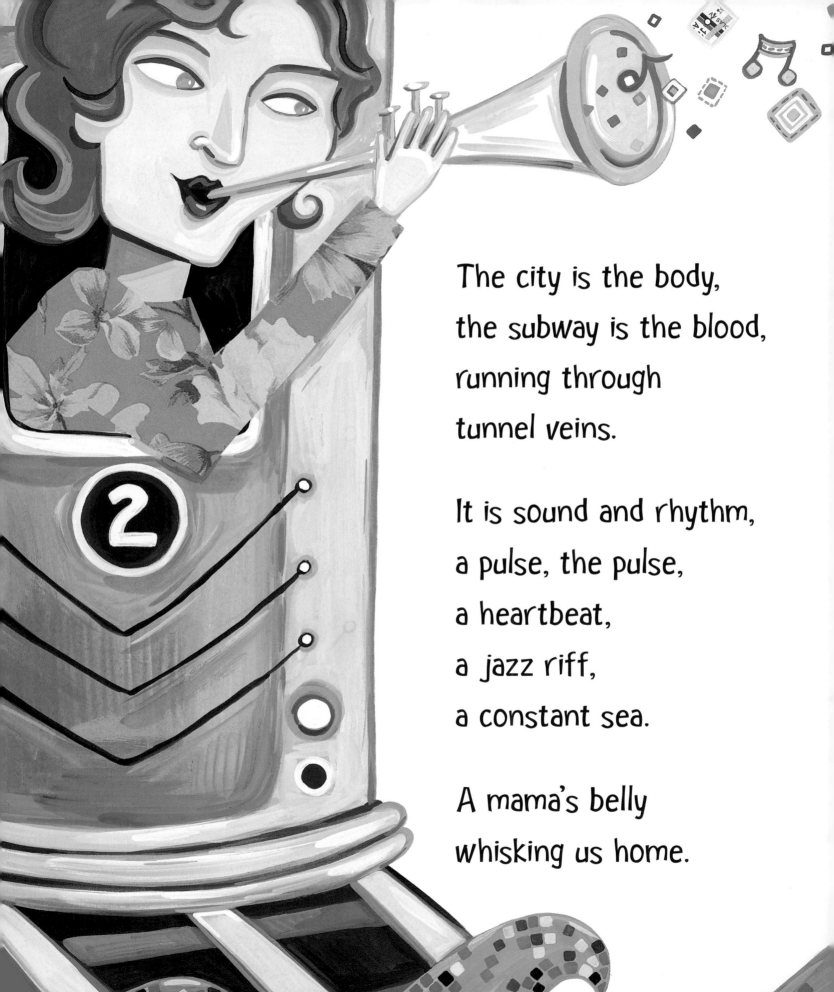

The city is the body,
the subway is the blood,
running through
tunnel veins.

It is sound and rhythm,
a pulse, the pulse,
a heartbeat,
a jazz riff,
a constant sea.

A mama's belly
whisking us home.

Welcome to the world
underground.
Tokens and turnstiles,
tickets to enter.
Please swipe your Metrocard.
Please swipe again.

Waiting for the train,

music in the station,

bucket drums

trumpet horn.

The beat and the wait and the rumble-growl,

a light in the dark,

a floating star,

squeak and squeal and screech to the stop.

ST. PENN STATION

Please stand
to one side—
off and in and in and out.
Stand clear of the closing doors.
The doors do close,
the music fades.
Now we're in
the time machine.

Standing, sitting
holding, hanging
snoozing, eating
reading, moving.

Cowboy hats and hip cats,
baseball caps and fur wraps.
A sea of faces,
an ocean of voices,
a bit of the world in every car.

Let's go!   *English*

Vamanos!   *Spanish*

An alé!   *Creole*

Poi'dem!   *Russian*

Zou ba!   *Chinese*

Brooklyn-bound or Queens-bound,
Manhattan-bound or Bronx-bound,
coming and going, going and coming.

The city is the body,
the subway is the blood,
running through
tunnel veins.

This is an express train,

a local train,

my train.

Uptown or downtown,

crosstown or out-of-town.

Next stop on this train is . . .

161st Street—
this is Yankee Stadium!
Boys of summer,
house that Ruth built,
take me out to the old ball game.
Pitch, smack
home run!
Next stop on this train is...

West Side, 81st Street—
Museum of Natural History.
Dinosaurs!
Stars in the day,
light in the night,
a whale flying overhead,
then a walk in Central Park.
Next stop on this train is...

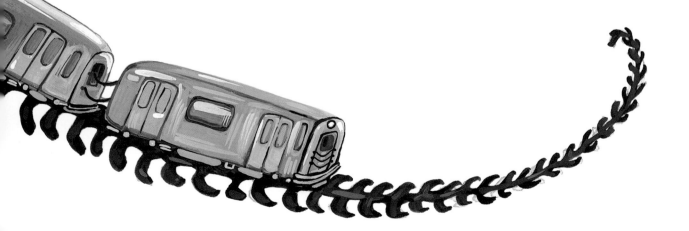

Coney Island,
Stillwell Avenue—
rattle of the Cyclone,
sticky cotton candy,
aquarium and ocean.
Tide comes in, tide goes out,
coming and going, going and coming.
Next stop on this train is...

Times Square, 42nd Street—
heart of the city
pumping its blood.
Transfer is available
to the N, the Q, the R, the S, the W,
the 1, the 2, the 3, the 7, the 9.

Language of the subway—

Do you speak it?

2 to the N,

7 to the Q,

A to the L to the 4 to the 6.

Letters and numbers,

colors and letters,

numbers and colors,

coming and going, going and coming.

Next stop on this train is...

THE TRAIN IS BEING HELD IN THE STATION

My stop,
my home.
A far-off island
lit by the moon.
The train stops,
the conductor speaks—
Red signals
up ahead.
Apologies
for any delay.

Standing, sitting
holding, hanging
snoozing, eating
reading, moving
to sound and rhythm,
a pulse, the pulse.

A heartbeat,
a jazz riff,
a constant sea.

A mama's belly
whisking us home.

Off the train,
up the stairs,
onto the stage,
into the light.

The city is the body,
the subway is the blood,
running through
tunnel veins.